To order additional copies of this book, contact:
Xlibris LLC
1-888-795-4274
www.Xlibris.com
Orders@Xlibris.com

Sadie
Loves Yoga

By Molly Schreiber

Illustrated by Joel Ray Pellerin

My name is Sadie and I
love to practice yoga!

With yoga, my life is brighter,
happier and much calmer.

Before I came to practice yoga,
my life was not this way.

I woke up grumpy in the morning.

I fought with my brother
and sister a lot.

I found school frustrating and boring.

I often felt jealous and envious of others who had more than me.

Inside, I just felt icky.

My first day of yoga, I didn't
know what to think.

All the other kids could breathe deeper,
balance longer, and just looked better.

Then I learned that yoga
was not a competition.

I learned it was a practice. I
learned that as we practice, we
get better each day. So I began
to practice almost every day!

I learned to take deeper breaths by
learning to quiet my mind and body.

I learned to balance better by
using a focal point and making my
mind stronger. I learned that this
is called using your third eye.

I am sure that I look better in my poses, but that does not really bother me because I know the practice is for me, and not for others to look at and see.

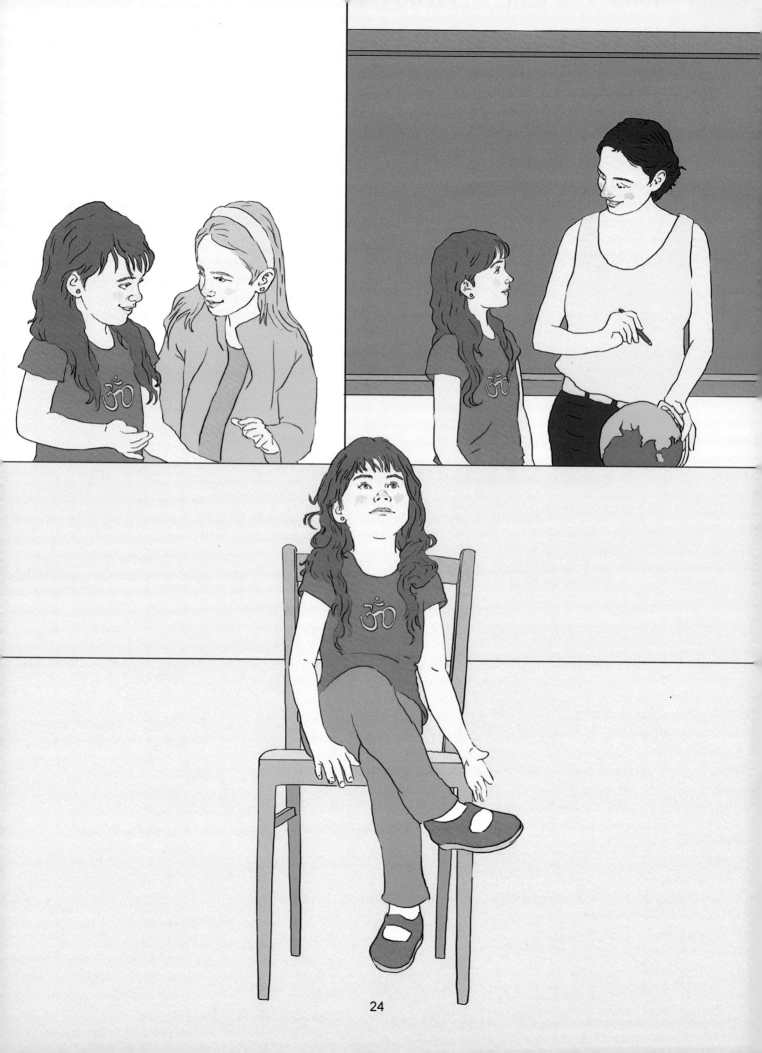

Today, with yoga, my life
is very different.

I enjoy each moment of my day
no matter what I am doing.

I stand taller.

I smile brighter.

And I stay calmer.

I practice my yoga every day
to be the best Sadie I can for
everyone I meet. Namaste!

Edwards Brothers Malloy
Thorofare, NJ USA
October 3, 2016